Tales from the Canyons of the Damned

PRESENTED BY USA TODAY BESTSELLING AUTHOR
DANIEL ARTHUR SMITH

Tales from the Canyons of the Damned No. 23

First Edition

Special thanks to Jessica West

ISBN-13: 978-1946777614 ISBN-10: 1946777617

Cover By Daniel Arthur Smith

Horror Fiction from Holt Smith ltd
Agroland
Tower

For Susan, Tristan, & Oliver, as all things are.

Mephisto
Hunter C. Eden

LIKE MANY HERO-VILLIAN PAIRS, Mephisto and the Daltons mirror each other. Through a glass darkly and all that.

Mephisto: Talkative for his kind; a flair for the dramatic; in league with strange powers, did he but know. By day, Mephisto lazes on the windowsill, recognizing with a single, lordly mew those who pass his perch. He is young, a year old at most, with a coat of deep black. Mephisto is of mixed breed, and the six toes on his right front paw disqualify him from competition, which requires pure blood and symmetry. This is probably why he was found abandoned under a Toyota as a kitten.

The Daltons: Talkative for their kind; a flair for the dramatic; in league with strange powers, did they but know. The Daltons are fat. He-Dalton carries the leisurely flab of a dreamer gone to seed, while She-Dalton slathered a generous layer of post-pregnancy weight over an already chunky foundation. Both Daltons consider themselves witches, though neither can honestly say that they have ever cast a working spell. What the Daltons can claim is tenacity. Witches, like mayflies, have short life-cycles. The time from a witch's pupation until conversion to Buddhism or born-again Christianity is profoundly brief. Whatever their failings, the Daltons have staying power.

He-Dalton and She-Dalton perform a Sabbath every Sunday. Mephisto watches from the top of a bookshelf with vague contempt. He-Dalton puts on a kimono while She-Dalton strips naked, gets down on all fours, and plays the altar. After fifteen minutes of wheedling the powers of darkness, He-Dalton roots around under the sagging hill of his stomach until he finds his cock, pumping until he squirts on She-Dalton. Lucifer never answers. Sometimes they try something new; She-Dalton nicks her breasts with a dagger or He-Dalton pisses on her trembling back-fat. They try to play it all off as just another religious tradition, like taking Eucharist or keeping kosher or meditating. Secretly, each hopes that maybe this time, if they chant just so, the floor will crack open and the fires will leap up, or the ceiling will split and a voice from on high will condemn them. Just this once, it won't be a day He-Dalton serves coffee and She-Dalton answers phones. God or the Devil—as long as somebody notices.

The balance between Mephisto and the Daltons would have remained a static *yin-yang* of vigilant disdain and stillborn daydreams except for two things:

First, the birth of Baby Dalton. He- and She-Dalton call Baby "Abramelin," or "Abram" for short. Mephisto just thinks of Baby Dalton as "the Skin Kitten," because it's little and loud and has no fur.

Second, the book. He-Dalton bought a little paperback (just a stack of typewritten pages bound into a pamphlet, really) entitled *On Other Skies*. He bought it because it looked like the sort of thing a real witch would own. It was.

"Hey, sulfur-pie," called He-Dalton to his wife as he pulled the book out of his backpack. "Come take a look at this!"

As he heard them talking, Mephisto knew his time had come.

Months before, huddled under the Toyota, shivering and crying for his mother or his litter-mates or anybody who could make the cold and hunger stop, Mephisto looked up to see a pair of torn old boots in front of him. "Kitten," said a deep voice, and a calloused hand reached under the car. The hand was warm, and Mephisto crawled into it, finding himself lifted up before a wide, black face with a bedraggled gray beard. Another hand rose like the night, covering the kitten's head and back, petting off the dry, cutting-cold flakes of snow. The biped grinned.

"Awful cold for you," he said. "Let's go somewhere else."

The old man lived under a bridge, a tangle of graffiti over his head and a fire at his feet. He drank from a bottle and gave Mephisto some roast beef from a paper plate.

"You and I, we got to be honest with each other," he said between sips. "The world don't give a shit about us, but you and I got to give a shit about the world."

Mephisto tore at the roast beef, angling his eyes at the man between bites. The old man pointed up.

"You look up at the sky, snowing like it is, and if you didn't know anything, you'd think that was how the sky always was—gray. But that's just the clouds."

He lowered his hand and gave Mephisto (who had no name yet) a pat between the ears.

"You take the clouds away, and there's just blue—wild blue yonder. Folks look at that and think it's the sky, but it ain't. Beyond that blue is outer space. And you probably thinking to yourself right now, *'That's* the real sky—couldn't possibly be no other.' But that ain't the sky any more than the clouds or the blue atmosphere."

The old man took a long swallow from his bottle.

"The *real* sky is somewhere else. Our sky rains and snows, and this real sky rains too, but the Rain is *alive*. When I came back home in '68, folks told me what I saw was on account of the bullet coming so close to my brain."

The old man paused, pointing at a long scar on his temple.

"But it's a vision," he continued. "Comes on me all at once and I faint. Used to be, I'd wake up and cry for hours."

Mephisto, warmer and fed, gave the old man a curious look.

"Not everybody can find their way to the True Sky, but those of us who can always know each other. Human beings, we go there in dreams or visions. Cats got their own way and dogs got their own way and every other one of God's creatures, if they get marked like you and I. Ain't something I wish on you, little cat, but it's going to happen. Maybe one day, you got to protect somebody from the Rain."

The old man drank deeply again and was quiet. Mephisto stared into the fire for a long time, sipping and watching until they both fell asleep. The next morning, the old man took him to the Humane Society, where the receptionist decided to call him Snickers. The Daltons took him in for his black coat and six-toed foot and absinthe-green glare and named him Mephisto. She-Dalton whelped Abramelin. He-Dalton found the book. It began.

On Other Skies said the promise of a human life could attract the attention of the True Sky, opening up vistas of knowledge for the offerer. It only required a dedication. No knives or burnt offerings—just a promise and a painted sign, for the Rain's master, the Sol Invictus, the Unconquered Sun of the True Sky, liked living flesh. He-Dalton and She-Dalton never really wanted a child, but they hadn't not wanted one badly enough to really take precautions. They loved Abramelin as much as they had the imagination to love anything, but like Mephisto, he was more of an accessory. Something to be shown off, minted a Satanic Dalton, and left to his own devices.

The Sign of Rain looked like a circle with three droplets inside it. She-Dalton painted it on the door of Abramelin's nursery while Mephisto watched. He-Dalton read the required verse in his most diabolic voice. It wasn't really a *sacrifice*. If it worked, it worked. If not, they would keep raising Abramelin in a properly witch-like way, send him off to college, and hope to Baal for the best. If the Rain didn't come, nobody needed to know. All parents make mistakes.

The Rain came. Mephisto heard it first—the distant sound of wind or breath and a splatter on glass of something too thick to be water. He had begun sleeping by the Skin Kitten's crib, and he looked out the window to see that the sky had turned the color of moss, filled with drifting clouds of half-burnt bodies. Things circled in the air like crows rough-hewn from gristle, swooping down to test the pane with their fleshy beaks. Always, the sound of breath on the wind.

That breathing triggered something in Mephisto. Nothing so definite as a memory, but a possibility, something that had always been inherent in him, if he thought about it. The old man dreamed his way to the True Sky, but Mephisto, should he wish, could travel a cat's path.

He-Dalton and She-Dalton were asleep, and even the Skin Kitten didn't wake up when Mephisto leapt up on the railing of the crib and down beside the baby. Cocking one blade-like ear, he listened to Abramelin's breath. There was something he could do with that breath, if he chose. Bipeds said his talent was murder, but the baby wouldn't die any more than the winds died from filling a ship's sails.

It came to him at once. Placing his nose gently against the baby's lips, Mephisto inhaled. Abramelin coughed and started to cry, but Mephisto was already away, leaping upwards past the ceiling and roof and clouds and space to where the True Sky began. Mephisto found himself drifting on a breeze filled with ash. Looking up, he saw roiling green sky and pulses of dim light, specks of floating jelly and sacs of meat borne on the wind.

"Oh, little cat," said a voice beside him. "I never wanted to see you here, but I knew I would."

Mephisto looked over to see the old man beside him, hovering amid clouds of ash and scorched limbs. He looked weaker, hands shaking and lips trembling, tears in his eyes. Like the first time they met, the air was cold. The charred clouds parted for a moment and Mephisto saw a vertical ocean of moving skin, scarred, pale blue, and curved slightly like the horizon.

"That there's the Sol Invictus," said the old man, willing himself to stay stationary against the wind. "It ain't the sun you and I know, but it wants to be. The more folks it gets, the closer it comes to rising over our world."

Great cysts bubbled up on the hide of the Sol Invictus, bursting for a few moments into light before settling back into red boils. Around it orbited rings of human bodies, bolts of electricity leaping from their torsos to that landscape of blue skin.

At once, Mephisto found himself gliding down into Abramelin's crib. Every night since, it's been a fight.

The Rain always arrives with the sound of breathing and the smell of ash. Mephisto lifts his head to see something like a headless dove perched on the edge of the Skin Kitten's crib. The dove-thing preens itself with long, human incisors set in the hole of its throat, grooming flat shards of bone rather than feathers. Flopping like a pigeon, it comes to rest next to baby Abramelin, and Mephisto is on it in one leap, burying his teeth in its ragged, bare neck. By the time He-Dalton is up to check on Abramelin, the body—bones and all—has already melted to a wet spot in the crib.

Mephisto sees He-Dalton's disappointment. He gets up every time Abramelin cries because he hopes this will be it, the day the world's lead flows into the mold of his dreams. A faint, stinking stain on the pillow. Spit-up. He'll clean it tomorrow. For his part, Mephisto feels no higher power guiding him, no gentle presence that leads him on. He kills the things from the True Sky for the same reason he lies next to Abramelin: because they are both little creatures, and the world will freeze them if it can.

Mephisto does what his kind have always done—he kills vermin. There are bigger things in the True Sky, but the smallest drops of Rain always fall first, so Mephisto does what he can to stop the storm early. Sometimes he sees the old man and sometimes he doesn't as he spends night after night tearing apart the rubbery hides of the Rain-things until his coat is covered in their greasy blood. By the time he returns to the crib, the blood is little more than a faint vapor and Abramelin is safe for the night. The rain always comes after dark, because the Sol Invictus cannot yet rise during the day.

Nights like that. Sometimes Mephisto gets hurt, sometimes not. The Daltons never notice either way. From familiar to decoration in six months.

Years pass. The Sign of Rain gets scrubbed away and He-Dalton and She-Dalton turn thirty, thirty-five. Abramelin goes to school and the kids make fun of his name. Nothing creative. It starts as "Abraham's Melon" then gets shortened to "Melons." At thirty-eight, He-Dalton and She-Dalton find Jesus. Maybe the job opening at a Christian coffee shop in need of an assistant manager is He-Dalton's ticket out of Starbucks. Maybe the Black Mass is getting hard on She-Dalton's knees. Either way, life rolls over but doesn't get up.

The Daltons deny, toss out, or burn anything hinting of the dishwater darkness of the Hell they courted for twenty years, give or take. Abram (his name officially changed now) is told that Mommy and Daddy were wrong for many years, and that Jesus, not Lucifer, is the good guy. Abram needs to remember this, for his salvation depends on it. He-Dalton and She-Dalton thank God every night for delivering them from the horrid sins of their past, opening a kingdom free of pain before their souls. Surely *this* was what they had hoped for all those years. He-Dalton gets a pentagram tattoo removed from his right shoulder. Mephisto is renamed Mittens. The Rain continues to fall.

It continues through Bible readings and church luncheons and youth groups for Abram, no longer a Skin

8

Kitten but a biped like the rest. One teary night, He-Dalton confesses his attempt to give his own baby to the powers of Hell. "To *think* what I did!" says He-Dalton, and Abram says it's okay. He's ten. What else would he say? Mittens keeps fighting.

One night in the True Sky, the Sol Invictus speaks to Mittens. It doesn't use words so much as a sensory intonation Mittens feels and understands through the light in his eyes and the air in his lungs.

Why do you bother? says the Unconquered Sun. *What are you given?*

The rings of twitching bodies around it have changed innumerable times, each one burning briefly to power the Sol Invictus's rays before adding its ash and unusable parts to the wind. Mittens ignores the voice, seeking out the old man when he can find him.

"It's you and me still," he says, swatting at the things that ride the wind with a heavy stick. When the winds allow them to get close enough, Mittens headbutts the old man affectionately, then they're thrown apart.

There is no reason, the Sol Invictus continues. *I could swat you into dust.*

Mittens is older and less maneuverable, but the Sol Invictus, for all its unstoppable incandescence, is slow. Its speed is that of the rising sun, not the stalking cat.

But Abram is getting faster and stronger. One night, he awakens as Mittens draws a lungful of breath from him. The boy pushes the cat aside, half-awake, and sees for a brief instant the swirling green sky straining to enter his window, the floating jelly-things in the Sol Invictus's orbit. He's a boy who lives in fear, who even at ten still runs to his parents' bedroom over nightmares.

"Mommy! Daddy!" he says. "There's something outside the window and Mittens is acting weird!"

He-Dalton puts a pillow over his head, but She-Dalton gets up to meet her son in the hallway.

"What did you see, sweetie?" she asks.

"Something outside the window," says Abram. "And Mittens had his nose in my mouth."

"Come on, honey," says She-Dalton. "Everything's all right."

She-Dalton waddles down the hallway as He-Dalton snores. She steps into Abram's room and turns the light on, blinking at its piss-colored harshness. Outside the window, the sky is still green. Something clings to the glass, reminding her of a flying squirrel that's been skinned and covered over with plastic wrap, all the little arteries in its belly pulsing against the window. Beyond, She-Dalton sees the slightest edge of the Sol Invictus. She remembers the Sunday night Black Masses, the years of blasphemy, and the Sign of Rain painted on Abram's door when they never expected anything to come of it.

"Jesus," she says. "Jesus save us…"

The window shatters and Mittens yowls as the Rain-thing glides down onto the carpeted floor. At once, He-Dalton is behind his wife and son, rubbing his eyes.

"God in Heaven," he says, the first sincere prayer he has uttered to any god in his entire life. The thing on the floor squeals and Mittens leaps on it, snapping the vertebrae of its neck through the spongy muscle. She-Dalton screams and He-Dalton pulls his family back, away from the door, leaving the Sol Invictus time to address Mittens in a booming voice the Daltons can't feel.

Why?

Mittens swats down something else that floats in through the window. Yet another drop of Rain. There is no reason. He does this for the same reason the old man did—because he is the only one who can.

You're not as fast as you once were, says the Sol Invictus. *There's a pain growing in you.*

Downstairs, the Daltons are praying frantically, and Mittens reflects on the Unconquered Sun's words.

The boy was given to me. You have twenty years, but I am eternal. Your body is broken by the very rays I shed. You are an annoyance to me, not an enemy.

The Daltons stay awake all night, skip work and school to pray. Mittens sits in Abram's room and thinks. He thinks about the way his skin burns, how the bottoms of his paws are cracking and his eyes blur. He knows something is changing in the Daltons. He has been familiar and housecat and ornament and now something else. "Why doesn't that cat leave the room?" asks He-Dalton, over and over. Maybe Mittens is more than just a tasteless purchase from ignorant days. Maybe their prayers were answered.

Without ceremony, He-Dalton throws Mittens outside, abjures him as an agent of Satan in the name of Jesus Christ Our Lord and Savior. He yowls and scratches at the door until He-Dalton comes back with a cross, then a BB gun. Abram is doomed.

Neither Mephisto nor Mittens now, he wanders, out again in the winter. For days he wanders. The stinging BBs in his back grow red and infected, each solitary shot knitting into a fever. Finally, shaking, he finds a heap of trash under a grimy bridge. There is no fire, no plate of roast beef, no warm pair of hands.

You never should have bothered, says the Sol Invictus in a voice that echoes through his burning skin, through his sluggish, fiery blood. Mephisto closes his eyes. They never open on that gray winter sky again.

"Little cat, I been waiting here for you," says the old man, his voice a bit stronger and younger now.

Mephisto opens his eyes and sees first the Sol Invictus, rings of bodies strung about it like beads. He feels warm hands around him and looks away from the Unconquered Sun to see the old man's wide, smiling face.

"I don't remember my last night," he says, cradling the heavy, blood-stained stick under one arm and stroking Mephisto's ears with the other. "I don't know if it's because I forgot or, because it was so much like all the other nights, it wasn't worth remembering. I don't know how long I been here, since there's no night. But I been waiting for you."

Mephisto will never see the newspaper article that describes how Abram disappeared from his bed. Suspicion lands on the Daltons, then flies away. Their church holds a fundraiser, but neither He-Dalton nor She-Dalton attend it. People will say in later years that the disappearance of their only son aged them, gave He-Dalton that haggard, pale look and stole the weight off She-Dalton until she became a trembling skeleton. Nobody finds Abram. A cold case.

"When I was a boy, I had a puppy died of the leukemia," the old man continues. "I went to church and asked the preacher if I would see that puppy in Heaven. He told me animals ain't born with souls—they only grow them from being around good people. I only had that puppy a month, and I wondered if that was enough time for it to grow a soul or not; I wondered if I was good enough to plant that seed. I was afraid to ask."

The old man seems less old now, and the Rain and the howling wind and the Sol Invictus seem slightly farther off.

You've wasted your years, it booms, but the voice no longer vibrates through their arteries, making their brains ache.

"During the day, I used to go read at the library. Some folks complained, but I was quiet and polite, so usually they left me in peace. I read about wars a lot, from all over history. I wanted to understand things I'd seen. Things I'd done."

He paused, and Mephisto no longer saw any gray in his hair.

"The Aztecs believed that they had to fight to keep another sun from rising and knocking ours out of the sky. If you was an Aztec, you needed a dog with you when you died. On the way to the hereafter, there was a river and you could only cross it on the dog's back. That didn't make sense to me when I read it. How you going to ride a dog across a river? But then I got back to what that preacher said. Maybe animals only do grow souls from being around us, but couldn't it also be the other way, too?"

You were beneath me in life, you are beneath me still, mutters the Sol Invictus, but its light is dimming and the chattering of the Rain is now a fading drizzle of whispers. The green sky darkens to a blackish-turquoise, but the man's strong arms hold Mephisto.

"We still got rivers to cross, little cat. Rivers upon rivers."

But as the True Sky's dusk winks at last into night, Mephisto sees the white sickle of his strong, youthful smile.

The Food Police
Lara Frater

"WITH A BMI OF 26, a muscle mass of 20% and a body fat of 28%, you are too fat to have ice cream—meatsack," the foodbot almost sang in a pleasant male voice. This particular one only delivered frozen treats. It looked like a metal man with painted on red hair wearing a cap with polka dots on it. Its face had a big grin with once pearly white teeth that had rusted to brown. The stomach opened after you ordered to deliver the treat. It was supposed to be retro, an ice cream server as they looked a hundred years ago.

Emma Dive wasn't pleasant and didn't care about retro or metal men. After a long hard day at work and temperatures ranging in the low-hundreds, she needed a lousy vanilla ice cream cone. Something to cool her off from her office job where she sat with twenty sweaty and stinky people in a small room at a small table with weakly rationed air conditioning. Emma spent the day in a sweat stained, mandatory, long-sleeved uniform that she stripped out of as soon as she left the building.

She hoped for enough food points. However, this stupid machine wouldn't give it to her because, according to her morning weigh-in, she was still at risk for obesity, making any high calorie food unobtainable.

The idea came to her to order something with fewer calories: ice cream without the cone.

"I'm sorry," the pleasant voice sang again. "With a BMI of 26, a muscle mass of 20% and a body fat of 28%, you are too fat to have ice cream. Now get on the treadmill, stupid!"

"You damn machine!" she screamed and punched it. The foodbot didn't respond except continued to make the stupid rusty grin. "Gimme my goddamn ice cream."

"Just move on, fatty!" said a male voice from behind her.

Emma resisted the urge the pummel both the foodbot and the guy behind her. She was hot. Sweat had formed in every place on her body. Her armpits felt like they stored an ocean and she didn't even want to think of the pools in the bottom of her bra. She wanted an ice cream and to go home, but that wasn't going to happen as long as she was "at-risk."

She took a deep breath. She ordered sugarless and fat-free lemon ices. Only ten calories a serving. The stomach opened. A cup came down and with a splat, crushed ice fell, then a yellow liquid squirted over it in a thin stream. It looked like the foodbot was peeing from its stomach all over her ices.

"Thank you! Enjoy your ices and remember nothing tastes as good as thin feels."

Emma grabbed her ices from the metal stomach and ignored the angry looks from the skinny people behind her. At least they looked as sweaty and miserable as she did.

When a woman vomited two persons back, the angry looks moved from Emma to her.

The woman was her age with a shrunk-in face indicating starvation but the loose folds of skin that fell out of her tank top revealed the history of a surgery. The woman's face looked youthful but her hair looked lifeless and limp. Her eyes had dark circles underneath and her cheeks had large, noticeable, red pimples.

When she fainted, no one moved to help her. They skipped her place in line. When she woke up, she would have to go to the back.

Emma turned away and tried to focus on her lemon ices which were really ice, lemon juice, and a package of Sweetopia which didn't taste "just like sugar" no matter what the commercials said. It wasn't as good as ice cream. Nothing was, but it at least cooled her off.

She walked to her apartment after spying long lines for the buses. Everyone got out at the same time but the company never had enough buses. While she wanted a quick way home, spying the long lines and thinking about standing among the hot and stinky made her decide to walk the mile instead. She needed the exercise anyway.

Since she had been "at risk" for some time, she could only buy food in small quantities. Emma was allowed to choose her own lunch from the office foodbot but she didn't have a lot of food points so there wasn't much of a selection. She usually ended up with a medium salad of mostly limp green leafy vegetables and some kind of soy cubes. Every morning, a truck delivered her breakfast along with that of five other people who lived in her building. It used to be six until Joe Goldstein from the fourth floor went crazy and attempted to break into the foodboxes. She remembered the morning she found him wild-eyed trying to open her foodbox with a sharpened pencil. She didn't report him as he hadn't gotten her breakfast and instead, had run off screaming when he saw her. Later that morning, the cops came and took him away, probably to the camps or maybe he got the surgery. Joe was larger than her but not by much. The thought of her trying to steal someone else's breakfast terrified her. She hadn't gotten to that point—yet.

Every evening, she found a dinner package waiting in her foodbox. The food came out of her salary. After deductions for her unhealthy tax, Emma brought home very little.

She felt lightheaded when she was entered the hot lobby of her apartment building. She perked up thinking of dinner. She hoped for something tasty at least. She unlocked the box with a keycard. And saw the tray with a plastic cover and a note written on top.

Warning At Risk for Obesity.
Dinner:
Skinless broiled chicken 3 oz.
Steamed asparagus.
1 small whole wheat potato with Butteresque.
One orange.
Calories: 400

Emma looked over the label twice before letting out a scream. "Goddamn it! I just want a single ice cream!"

"Well you ain't getting it, you fat cow!" someone from an upper floor yelled. It sounded like Mrs. O'Brien, a notorious eavesdropper and snitch and the person who had probably told the cops about Joe. "Now shut up or I'll call the cops."

The last thing she needed was a visit from the Food Police. Emma rarely went to her weight system meetings and when she did, she didn't participate. She sat silently in her chair, listening to people crying and saying how desperate they were to lose weight. The group leader would try to motivate them by saying if they didn't fix their weight, they would not only die young, but suffer all kinds of ailments. Emma found the meetings boring, except the one time this fat woman went crazy. But because of a food shortage, they were all forced to lose weight.

Emma remembered when she was young, her mother worried about her getting fat. Her grandmother assured her it was common for kids to get chubby. Her mother put her on a weight loss plan anyway. It didn't work. She ended up gaining more weight and had struggled to be thin ever since.

For months she had been on the mandatory weight loss program—a requirement for her job—but so far, she hadn't lost so much as a pound.

She opened the door, put her things down on her desk and went straight to her couch. She was exhausted. Her apartment was simply furnished. One large room contained the living room, dining area, and breakfast nook. Adjacent was her bedroom with just enough space for a twin bed and a dresser. She tossed her dinner tray on the couch with no intention of eating it at the table. The building's AC was rationed, making it only slightly cooler than outside. Her plan was to eat and veg out until bed.

"Attention, fatso!" a male voice yelled. The same voice of the Foodbot but this time, more stern. It was the online reminder service, an interactive computer in every household that acted like a personal assistant and monitoring program. "You are at risk for morbid obesity. You must exercise for one hour or else you will die of cancer and heart disease."

"I exercised at work."

"Negative, indication of only 30 minutes exercised logged, blobbo."

"I walked from work to home."

"That doesn't count, idiot."

"I'll exercise after dinner."

"That is acceptable, tubby. I will remind you in a half-hour. Remember, it's all your fault."

Emma gobbled her tasteless dinner. Dry chicken with overcooked vegetables. The potato, crossed-bred with whole wheat, tasted terrible and the sorry excuse for fake butter didn't help. She consumed the too small orange and wished for more. In about five minutes, she finished, but was still hungry. Instead of turning on her TV, she went to her bedroom, flopped down on the bed, reached into the hollow hole in her box spring and pulled out something from her emergency stash—mostly snacks she had taken from thin friends who would never notice them missing. She envied her friend Alicia who was slim and could buy all the food she wanted. Alicia used to buy extra food for her, but that stopped when it became a felony to give food to at risk people.

Emma nibbled on some peanuts. She felt a little better but still wanted ice cream. She would go to sleep but she knew her alarm system would wake her in a half hour, screaming insults at her until she exercised.

Her thoughts were interrupted by her doorbell. Emma went to the front door and checked the videocom. A single food cop waited outside. The day got worse. It was already too late to pretend she wasn't home because the cop would know she'd checked the videocom.

Emma opened the door. The white man, very thin and slightly older than Emma, didn't smile. He wore a blue uniform with a patch that had the EAC—Eating Action Coalition, which everyone called the food police—logo on it. He carried what looked like a cooler. "What can I do for you, Officer?"

"May I come in, Miss Dive?"

"Sure." She didn't want to look suspicious. She hoped he wasn't here to search the place. She thought of the hollow hole in her box spring. Had she remembered to cover it up? "Although, I have to exercise soon."

"I won't be long." He came in and looked around the place.

"Would you like some water with lemon? I'm afraid I'm dieting now, so I don't have much to offer."

"It isn't a diet," he said, his voice sterner than any computer. "That's an obsolete word. It's a weight management system and lifestyle change. No wonder you've failed at losing weight."

"Yes, you're right." Emma found the best way to deal with the cops was to agree with anything they said.

The cop walked into the kitchen. Emma had stopped cleaning it a long time ago. It was dusty and didn't look like it had been touched. It wouldn't be as long as Emma remained at risk.

"So what brings you here? It isn't my upstairs neighbor, is it? She calls on everyone. Honestly, I worry about her. The poor thing never has anyone visit. I think she wants attention."

"This is a courtesy call. Your name popped up in a random sweep. We've noticed you've missed some exercise and have been trying to get food when you don't have enough points."

"Oh well, you know. I'm not always sure how many points I have. And I come home from work and I'm tired—" she paused, "and hungry."

The cop ignored her last statement. "What about the mornings? You don't always exercise before work."

"I work long hours. I always do my two minutes of calisthenics. But I was just about to finish my exercise for the day." She hoped her alarm system would go off to save her for a change, but it remained silent.

The officer went to his cooler. He opened it up and took out a wrapped ice cream bar.

"You want this, don't you?"

Emma didn't respond. This had to be a trick.

"Well, do you want one?"

"This is entrapment."

"Nonsense. I don't like to send people to the camps because they crave something. Now, do you want it?"

"Yes."

"Good. Human beings have cravings. That's normal, but what makes us different from the animals is we can say no."

"No!"

"Good."

"No!" Now she understood why Joe went crazy. The heat, the lack of food, the rationed AC. She was about at her breaking point. "Give me that goddamn ice cream!"

The man sighed. "Emma, what have you learned? Obviously nothing." He waved the ice cream bar in front of her like a magic wand.

"Give it to me. I want an ice cream and that's it. What the hell is wrong with that? I don't want ten of them."

"You're obese."

"So what? Every time I do my medical scans, everything is normal."

"Those don't mean anything. In the future, you will get cancer, heart disease, and diabetes. Do you want me to show you pictures?"

She didn't respond.

He looked frustrated. "I'm going to give you a citation. Increase your exercise to two hours a day and lower your calorie intake by 300."

As he went to grab his pad, he put the ice cream on the counter. Emma went for it, but the cop was faster; he grabbed her by one of her wrists.

"We must learn to resist temptation, Emma. You don't want to end up at the fat camps or with mandatory surgery, do you?"

Emma felt something stir inside her. She didn't know what. No ice cream? More exercise? Only 900 calories a day? A threat to go to those torturous camps? Surgery that killed one out of every hundred people? Or made you look like the pimply girl from the cold treats line?

Emma didn't think. She used her free hand to punch him hard in the face. The cop, who hadn't expected the blow, released her hand.

Emma used that moment not to grab the ice cream, but to nab a kitchen knife off the dusty rack.

"Miss Dive, what—"

The cop didn't have a chance to finish. He was so used to compliance that it astonished him when Emma embedded the knife in his chest. He stared at the wound and the blood gushing out of it. He looked at Emma, stunned, then crashed to the ground.

She picked up the ice cream and unwrapped it. It was very delicious—cold, followed by sweet and creamy vanilla, her favorite. It slid down her throat and brought her into rapture. She wanted to eat it slowly but her hunger took over and she ate it in four glorious bites. All of the day's events went away. She felt less stressed and even less hot.

"Attention," a stern male voice said.

"Yes, I know, it's time to exercise."

A wall opened and a treadmill came down like a murphy bed. Emma got on it and began walking, thinking of the ice cream. She remembered the cop had a cooler, which meant the potential for more ice cream.

Now that she'd had the ice cream, she enjoyed her walk. Her thoughts became clearer. As she exercised, Emma tried to think of the best way to get rid of the body.

The Three Ds
C.C. Ameel

It's coming but I feel no Dread;
That comes from others, not from my head.

I see their fear, sorrow, and remorse.
It's not for me, but for them, of course.

My time is near, but theirs will come too.
We all have an end; some later, some soon.

They listen, confused by my cheerful refrains,
And I realize that we were never the same.

But the prime of your life, cut short! they say.
Please, save your breath; I've looked forward to this
day.

Yet I calm myself so as not to reveal,
All the anticipation I now feel.

Though today is my last, I must pretend,
That I'm not happy I've reached the end.

I should be afraid; it's normal, they say.
As they gather around me, hold hands, and pray.

I sigh, relieved I'd soon hear no more,
And close my eyes to search for the door.

A stymied breath, then Death at last.
My future is gone, but not my past.

There is dark, there is cold, then there's release.
At last, I can say I've finally found peace.

My time has come, no more thoughts to stray,
At last, I'll gladly meet Decay.

Where will it start? I can only surmise,
Hoping for a fantastic surprise.

A tingle, vibrations, exhilaration,
I feel so alive in all my desolation.

More alive in Death than ever in life.

Each second, I'll lose another part of me,
Don't mourn my loss; it's a joy, you see.

I seek Decay, and it's found me.

Alas, a happy ending was not meant to be.
Abruptly, flames surrounded me.

If my lungs bore air, you'd hear me scream;
This cruel fate was not my dream.

I've no recourse, I've no recourse.
Now, suddenly, I understand their remorse.

Remorse, though they plotted to betray,
To take away my long-lasting Decay.

There's nothing left; I've been condemned.
And Dread? It found me, in the end.

Ash
Ian Garner

MY FIRST DAY OF SUMMER STARTED out well enough. It was a warm day in May; not too hot, but you needed gills to navigate the humidity. Freshman year had been hell on my GPA and metabolism, but I had plans to celebrate with copious amounts of cheap booze and pizza rolls at my friend Jerry's place.

My girlfriend at the time, Amanda Marie Saunders, had other plans.

"Bobby, I told you I don't like it when you hang out with Jerry. Last month, I had to drive you home at 2 A.M. the night before my lab practical."

"And because you love me, you were happy to do it."

"You puked on my favorite pajama bottoms. Those weren't cheap."

"Calm down, I already bought you new ones."

"Yeah, but those were sentimental."

After about ten minutes of arguing, I put my balls in a mason jar, called Jerry to cancel our plans, and got in the truck to drive Amanda home. She was very persuasive when she wanted to be.

"Dad's gonna be gone tonight," she told me as we merged onto the interstate.

"Oh yeah?"

She turned in her seat to face me, her hand slowly gliding over to my right leg. "Mmhmm. He flew out to Denver this morning for a meeting. Shouldn't be back for another few days."

My heart raced a little faster. A chill ran down my back. Not from fear, though maybe I ought to be afraid, considering I was pushing 90 mph. "Interesting." I took the first exit I saw, not the correct one, but the most convenient one to get us off the road.

"I thought you might agree," she whispered in my ear. I shut down the engine and leaned back in my seat. Uncle Kracker played on the stereo, and like him, I closed my eyes to get lost in rock and roll and drift away.

The fireball in the rearview mirror stopped us. Well, maybe not the fireball itself, but the things that came with it. Seconds before, I felt the air around us move back as if suctioned. I chalked it up to, well, you know. But then the horizon turned a blood-red, and the Earth rocked with the force of the impact.

"What the hell was that?" Amanda asked. The window shattered immediately after. Glass flew like a thousand razors, and Amanda suddenly became a pincushion.

Think about that. One minute, you're getting post-finals victory lovin', and the next, your girlfriend turns into a porcupine. The sky is literally on fire, your truck looks like The Hulk kicked it down a hill, and your ears are bleeding. And Mom said college was supposed to be the easy part of life.

I crawled out of the truck, my ears ringing. Amanda fell out of the truck, her body limp and bloody. Her eyes were glazed over, and if it weren't for the rivulets of blood running down her neck, she might have looked at peace. I stumbled to my feet and turned to look at the chaos around me.

The mushroom cloud to the south was dissipating. *C'mon, Bobby, think. Remember the thumb trick Dr. Morris taught you?* I held my thumb up to the cloud; my thumb covered it, so I was at least safe from the flames. The wind was picking up, however, and wind meant fallout. *Get moving before you die, idiot.*

The truck was parked near a corn field, just out of view of the interstate. I tried to crank it up, desperate to get out of there. The engine didn't turn over. I had no choice but to trudge up the gravel road and back toward the exit, hoping to flag down a driver. What I found was a mess: cars piled up on the interstate, some already on fire. Those that weren't terribly damaged by the shockwave were still occupied by angry drivers, yelling, cursing, and spewing hatred at the people blocking their progress. I ran up to the first man I saw, an old farmer from the look of his tanned skin and faded overalls. The windows of his truck hadn't shattered, though they were a little cracked, and his engine still purred. He was arguing with a young man, a lawyer who smelled of Daddy's money and privilege. My ears were too rattled to understand what they were saying, but the young man kept pointing to his Cadillac.

"I can help push it out of the way!" I said. Well, I yelled. I had to, I couldn't hear otherwise.

The two men looked at me the same way they would a leper. Granted, my arms and legs were bleeding and my ears were clotting with blood, so I suppose they were entitled to their stares. The old man, bless his heart, yelled as loud as he could, but I only heard a whisper. I had to read his lips to catch what he said.

"I'd be much obliged."

The young man ushered us over to the car as he removed his jacket and sat behind the wheel. The old man next to me held up three fingers, then two, then one. When he dropped the last finger, we shoved the vehicle to get it rolling. It took us three good shoves before it rolled over to the shoulder, and the young man shook our hands. I'm going to assume he thanked us, but I can't be sure.

The farmer turned to his truck. "Wait!" I called after him. He turned to me, annoyed. "I need a ride to Northbrook!" Northbrook was a subdivision north of town. Amanda lived there. If I could make it there, I might be able to load up on food and water before heading to the courthouse. Back in the '50s, all the government buildings downtown were fitted with rubber seals around the doors and windows in case of dirty bombs or large-scale nukes. Granted, that was almost seventy years ago, but it was a better place than the interstate.

"Get in the truck. I'm headed just east of there. I'll drop you off," he said, or something like that. I was never too good at reading lips. I ran to the passenger door and climbed in. "Ain't you got a car?" he asked.

"Truck's dead!"

"Ain't no need to yell, son, I'm right here." We cruised down the highway much quicker than should have been legal. Emergency vehicles passed us on the other side, hurtling toward ground zero.

"Sorry!" I pointed to my ears, now crusted with blood. He seemed to relax a bit after that.

We turned onto the exit Amanda and I were intending to find, taking the north road up to her house. We drove past old, poverty stricken neighborhoods now in the throes of nuclear Armageddon.

The old man pulled into a long gravel driveway about three miles from Amanda's house. The truck rumbled up to an old farmhouse. Or what was left of one anyway.

"No, no, no, Suzanne!" The old man yelled as he jumped out of the truck. I climbed out too, in awe of and panicked by what I saw. During the shockwave, the tractor that sat not far away from the house had been picked up and shoved right through the kitchen. The wall was completely torn down and the rest of the house was in shambles. The old man rushed in, climbing over the tractor, digging through the rubble for, I presumed, his wife.

I found her in the rubble of the living room. "Over here!" I yelled, standing over the body. The staircase to the second floor had collapsed and buried her underneath, probably killing her instantly. The old man and I shoved the rubble off of her and he sat on his knees, rocking her back and forth.

I stood outside, giving him a moment's peace. I allowed myself a moment to think, fully realizing what had happened. An hour ago, I was finishing my last exam of the year. Now, I was running from nukes.

Holy Hell.

The smoke pulled me from my reverie. I looked up at the tree line, to the blood-red sky where the nuke had struck. In the panic, I hadn't considered that fire would be spreading. Sure enough, the forest before me had become an inferno to rival Hell itself, devouring everything in its path with righteous judgment. I turned on my heel, bolted over rubble and ash, and grabbed the old man's arm, yanking him away from his wife. "We have to go now!"

I thought he'd try to kill me then, judging from the pain and anger in his eyes. When he looked past me and toward the fire, his gaze became less fierce. In fact, I'd say it was calm. Resigned. At peace. I'll never forget what he did after that, not 'til the day I die. Instead of grabbing my hand, he slammed his keys in it. "Go. Take the truck. You'll need it more than me."

I didn't understand at first. "C'mon, mister, we have to go!" He just shook his head, then turned back to his wife, then back to me.

"Life ain't worth fighting for without her. Now git!"

I ran. God forgive me, I ran. I reached the truck just as the flames reached the pines only twenty yards from the house. I revved the engine, slid it into first, and I bolted down the old gravel driveway without looking back. I tore onto the main road and headed north, racing the flames. As I sped away, I glimpsed in the rearview mirror as the flames engulfed the old farmhouse.

I'm not convinced I did the right thing.

I raced north, heading for the river a few miles away from Northbrook. It wasn't the fastest route, but I figured the highway would be congested with vehicles and I didn't care to burn up in a traffic jam.

I raced across Parkman's Bridge just as the flames were about to catch me. A quick look in the rearview mirror revealed the pine trees on the bank of the Whitehelm River catch fire. The flames lashed out to lick the crimson sky and black clouds of smoke and radioactive ash filled the air. I stopped the truck and sat in awe of the destruction behind me. The river kept the flames on the south side of the bridge, and for the first time since the bomb fell, I stopped to ponder what the hell had happened.

Oh God.

Amanda.

As the firestorm raged, so did my anger. How could someone so young, so bright, so full of life just…die? Who could do that? Why?

The second bomb snapped me from my reverie. The mushroom cloud filled the air to the east and for a moment, I thought the sun had risen again in an instant. Granted, it was maybe 4:00 PM, but I swear, I've never seen anything so bright in all my life. This bomb was closer than the first, maybe half a mile closer than the initial blast compared to my position then. I scrambled to get in the truck and buckled in just as the shockwave sent the truck tumbling into the river.

Nukes: 2. Me: 0.

I don't know how long I was unconscious, but the heat of the flames on the south side of the bank woke me up. Luckily, the truck landed in the shallow end of the river, so I wasn't in danger of drowning. The real problem was the glass spear in my right thigh. When the truck flipped, glass flew everywhere, much like my own truck had done earlier that day. The metal was warped and the door was folded like an accordion. There was no way I was going to open that thing. I woke up groggy and disoriented, most likely concussed. I didn't hurt. At least, not immediately.

My left arm exploded with pain as I reached to unbuckle the seat belt. When I looked down, I saw my radius jutting out like a bloody spike. I won't lie—I puked. After thoroughly emptying my stomach, I unclipped the seat belt with my bruised but relatively unscathed right arm. Luckily, the windshield blasted out cleanly during the wreck, so I was able to shimmy out and down the hood of the truck. The movement sent a wave of pain through my leg, but considering I had to choose between burning alive or whining like a bitch for a while, I figured I could power through the pain for a bit longer.

I slid down the hood on my back and rolled into the river. Ever been in a river between two nuclear explosions? I don't recommend it. Usually the Whitehelm is a cool seventy-five degrees in the summer. It was a pretty nice swimming spot back when I was a kid. Unfortunately, the present conditions changed that a bit. I landed ass first in a steaming cesspool, which does wonders for a gaping hole in the arm. If I had to guess, the water temperature was closer to 150 degrees, but I don't really know for sure.

I struggled to stay afloat as the water poured into my wounds. The heat of the water shocked my system, and I think my heart may have skipped a beat. I struggled to stay afloat as the current caught me, dragging me downstream at breakneck speed. I distinctly remember thinking, *This is it. This is how I die.* I remember lying back, barely afloat, looking up at the sun one last time before smoke and ash covered it for a decade-long nuclear winter. *This isn't so bad.* I thought of the old man and his wife. I thought of Amanda. I thought of her smile when I picked her up that afternoon. I closed my eyes and, for the first time since Armageddon, I smiled and waited to die.

I woke up again on the bank of the river, just a few yards behind Amanda's house. The current had carried me maybe a mile away from the crash, and I woke up covered in algae and river funk. I forgot about the pain for a while as I lay there on my back, watching the clouds gather to blot out the sun. *Goddamn it. You failed Trig and now you can't even die properly.* The pain in my arm slowly crept back, and I realized that maybe I should get off my ass and find something to wrap my wounds. I rolled over and knelt on my left leg, pushing myself up and screaming as my right leg stretched out to bear a little of my weight. I hobbled over to the clay wall carved out by the river and grasped an old oak root poking through the dirt. *All right, you lazy sack of shit. Amanda would have climbed this hill ten minutes ago.* I gripped the root with my right arm and kicked against the clay with my left foot. I managed to prop my left elbow on the grass just beside the oak trunk and heave myself up despite the pain. I was feeling pretty good about myself until the glass shard in my leg hit a lump of clay and dug deeper into my muscles. I nearly fainted when I saw her, her long red hair gently blowing in the breeze, eyes bright and blue, full of passion and fury.

"I swear, Bobby, you can't do anything for yourself, can you?" Amanda grabbed my right hand and tugged, pulling my limp body over the edge of the cliff and onto the grass.

"Is this real?" I moaned as she rolled me onto my back.

"You tell me. It's your life." She knelt down beside me and stuck two fingers into the hole in my leg. "But first, close your mouth. This is gonna hurt like a bitch." With a quick tug, Amanda grabbed the glass shard and pulled it out of the muscle and dropped it onto the grass beside my knee.

I wasn't sure whether I should thank her or cuss her out, but the pain took me and the world became black before I could choose.

I woke up on a kitchen floor to find the red-headed woman standing over a stove. There was a pot on the burner, and my savior appeared to be cooking.

"Where am I?" I asked as I struggled to get up. The pain in my leg told me that was a bad idea, so I propped myself on my right elbow instead.

"The Saunders' house. Northbrook." The woman stirred the pot and pulled what appeared to be a cloth from the steaming water. "Now quit talking. You need to be resting."

"I've taken two or three involuntary naps today. I think I can stay awake a while."

"It wasn't today. I fished you out of the river a week ago."

"What?"

The woman turned around and I nearly puked. Instead of a face, she had...well, I really can't begin to describe it. If you've ever seen folks that had acid splashed on them, you'd understand what I mean. Where this lady should have had a face, there were only strips of flesh covering exposed muscle and bone.

"Holy hell!" I screamed. I kicked and scooted my way back across the floor until my back hit the cabinet on the far wall.

"Calm down," she growled. "I'm not gonna eat you."

"Damn right you're not!"

The woman/thing set the pot on the floor between us, reached in, and wrung the water from one of the rags. "Give me your arm. The broken one."

Naturally, I was a little hesitant to offer this demon lady my arm, but I had to allow my rational mind to sit in the cockpit for a moment. If she meant me harm, she wouldn't have helped me out of the river. If I really had been out for a week and she did want to eat me, I wouldn't be alive to process that terrifying notion. Furthermore, only Bond villains wait until their victim is awake to monologue about their diabolical plan. Besides, she reached over to grab my wrist anyway, and I was in no position to fight back. I let my guard down and allowed her to clean the wound.

"Who are you?" I asked.

"I figured you wouldn't recognize me. I'm Rosalind. Remember?"

I remembered the first time I went over to Amanda's house, maybe two years ago. Her father had hired a gardener to spruce the place up a bit, and she had worked dutifully to make the Saunders' home the prettiest in the cul-de-sac.

"I remember. What the hell happened to you?" I cringed a bit as she wrapped my arm in the bandage, but I can't deny, it felt pretty good after a minute.

"I was in the garden when the bombs fell. The first one didn't affect the neighborhood, but everyone jumped in their cars and sped off like madmen, heading God knows where. My cell phone died and I couldn't reach out to Amanda. I thought my best bet was to stay inside, maybe wait to see if help would come. So I went back inside.

"I made the mistake of walking out into the garden when the second bomb fell. It was closer, hotter. I remember feeling searing pain and heat, then nothing. The river killed the flames before they reached the house, thank God, but the damage was done. Windows shattered, trees fell, everything with a battery or power cord died. I was fortunate enough to get the backup generator running after I found you."

I looked down to notice another bandage on my leg where the glass shard had been. "What happened to your face?" I asked before I could catch myself.

"Ah...yes." I could see I had hurt her by asking. "When the second bomb fell, when the radiation and heat swept through, I was hit. My skin seared and my hair fell out. I found this wig in a neighbor's house while scavenging for food." She swiped at a tear trying to escape. "This morning, I also found sixteen lumps on my chest."

"Jesus," I began.

"No. This was no act of God. This was the folly of man." Rosalind coughed and heaved, and I scooted over to avoid being a radioactive barf bag. She wretched, green bile and crimson blood pouring forth from various holes on her face.

I felt a twinge of pity, but deep down, I had a horrific thought. *Good, good. The fewer people to feed, the better.* I shook my head, clearing the thought. I reached out with another cloth to allow her to clean up and preserve whatever dignity she had left.

"Thank you. Now, I must ask, where is Amanda?"

I hung my head and my heart hammered in my chest. "I'm sorry," I finally managed to croak. "She didn't make it."

Rosalind heaved and wretched again, this time with more blood than bile. "Perhaps...perhaps it's better that way. At least she won't have to endure the harsh remnants of this world like we'll be forced to do." A slight trembling quickly evolved to full-out shaking. Shakes soon turned to convulsions. The invasive thought returned. *Don't move. Let her go. She's not your problem, never was.* Within seconds, Rosalind was gone.

I managed to drag her body out behind the house and roll her off the cliff and into the river. It only took an hour. With my leg being screwed up, I thought I'd made decent time. I hobbled back inside, found a can of beans, and dumped them into a pot on the stovetop. I warmed them, poured them into a bowl, and sat down at the kitchen table to enjoy a quiet meal.

It's funny, really, how quickly you can go insane. It starts as a tickle in the back of your mind, a tiny sliver that scratches and claws its way into the forefront of your subconscious. It only takes a few days of total silence before you completely go bonkers.

I really ought to thank you. I spent, I don't know, three months? Four, alone? I can't really tell. The sky stays so damn cloudy, I can hardly see the moon at night. Anyway, I spent those first few months alone, scavenging around the neighborhood for food and supplies. I ate like a king those first few weeks. Steak, chicken, sautéed vegetables, you name it.

But then the generator ran out of gas. That was the end of hot meals for me, but I mean, there was still plenty of beef stew to eat from cans. I went through those a little too quickly, I think. After the second month, I had nothing but green beans and Spaghetti-Os. That was rough, but I guess better than nothing.

I started bathing in the river when my hair started falling out. The ash started raining pretty soon after Rosalind died, and the radiation poisoning followed pretty close behind. I'm lucky, I guess, because I look a hell of a lot better than she did. After all, I still have a face. I think. At least, that's what Amanda tells me. I see her a lot when I sleep in her room. She always stares at me and tells me I should have kept driving, but I just laugh and tell her she's bleeding from her neck down. She doesn't stick around long after that.

I was in a bad place until you showed up. I remember lying in her bed when I heard you howling outside the window. I crawled out of bed and limped over to the kitchen to open up a can of beans for you. You were such a good doggy, yes you were. I set that can of beans down on the porch and you came over and ate the whole thing in under a minute. You were so small, weren't you? So frail and bony, you could be my twin.

Oh, but you aren't so small now, are you, boy? No, you're Daddy's fat little man now.

Fat. Plump. Juicy.

You've been such a good listener for Daddy these past few weeks. That's it, come give Daddy kisses. Yes sir, such a happy boy.

So hungry…

Oh, you're just a wonderful friend for Daddy. That's right, come here, come sit with Daddy.

Quit stalling, Bobby, do it already.

Daddy's been so hungry lately. You've been such a good boy, Daddy's fed you extra and hasn't been eating much for himself. Oh, it's okay. You like being scratched behind the ears, don't you? Yes you do.

So close…

That's it. Daddy loves you, puppy. Yes he does. You're such a good boy. Such a cute, fat, juicy boy…no, stop. Stop that. Quit squirming. I said stop, damn it! Quit whining. Shhh, shhh. Look at me. Look at my eyes. No, don't kick. That's it. Look Daddy in the eyes.

Crack!

Yes, you've been a good friend to Daddy. Such a good friend. Now you get to take care of Daddy a little while longer. Need to get a fire going, get some salt and maybe some oregano. Yes, you'd go nice with a little oregano. Such a good boy.

Cough.

Where'd I put that knife?

Cough.

Ooh, a little blood with that one. Whoops, gotta clean that up. Oh, hey Amanda. Hungry? No? Okay, well, that's fine. I've got plenty I can cook up if you change your mind. What's that? Oh, that's my buddy. Such a good boy, yes he was. Listened to all my stories and everything. Yes, even the one about you dying. Oh, come on, you're not still mad at me for that, are you? Come on, babe, let me cook for you. Hey, Amanda, stop. I'm not kidding. Ow, that hurt! Amanda, no, I'm serious. Amanda. Amanda, why are the trees on fire? Did another bomb fall? Amanda. Amanda, you're scaring me. No. No, Amanda, put the glass down. I'm sorry, ok, I'm sorry! Listen, babe, let me cook you dinner! We can talk about this! No, I'm not jumping off that cliff, there's fire down there! Oh my God, Amanda, what the hell? Is that? No. No, you're not serious. Amanda, please!

Amanda?

Hello?

Are you there?

…Amanda?

Lost Tapes–
Aubrey Blackburne
Daniel Arthur Smith

"Recording begins with today's date, May 5th, 2018. My name is Agent Melissa Muldoon. Present with me is Agent Lawrence Meyer. Commencing interview of one Professor Aubrey Blackburne. Professor Blackburne, can you please state your name for the record?"

"My name is Aubrey Blackburne, Doctor Aubrey Blackburne."

"Thank you. Do you prefer Doctor to Professor?"

"Professor is fine. Whichever makes you comfortable."

"You referred to yourself as Doctor."

"I know. I was thinking I should be formal. For the interview. But I never really use it. The Doctor title, I mean."

"Do you normally go by Professor?"

"I go buy Aubrey, Miss Aubrey sometimes. But yeah, that's what the kids call you. Even before your doctorate."

"Before?"

"Since I was a TA."

"So Professor Blackburne then?"

"Yes. Sorry."

"Thank you for meeting with us. We appreciate when members of the community such as yourself come forward."

"Oh, anything I can do to help."

"When you called, you said you had information pertaining the disappearances—"

"The disappearances. Yes."

"Could you please be more specific? For the record."

"I'm here to talk about the disappearance of the Carmichael girl and the Christensen boy."

"Thank you, and can you tell me if you recognize the child in this photo?"

"Yes. That's little Sophia Carmichael."

"Thank you, and this one?"

"Hmmm. So sad. That's Lyndon Christensen."

"For the record, Professor Blackburne has identified Sophia Carmichael, age eight, and Lyndon Christensen, also age eight. Both missing since last week. Professor, why did you say, 'so sad'?"

"Well, it is. Isn't it? I mean for their parents, and everyone else. I saw them on the news. Heartbreaking, really. Don't you think?"

"Yes, I do. Can you tell me what information you have that brought you here today?"

"Yes. Of course. I know what happened to them."

"You know the whereabouts of these children?"

"No. No I don't. Not exactly. But I do know what happened to them. You see, I live in Branson Hall, right behind the playground."

"Did you see what happened?"

"I saw them playing there. Every day after school. That's where it happened."

"What did you see?"

"Agent Muldoon, do you know what a meme is?"

"Sure. Cat pictures, that sort of thing, something that goes viral on social media."

"Yes. That's a meme in its simplest form. A humorous image, spread across the internet from one person to another. But more precisely, it's an element that may be passed from one individual to another by nongenetic means, especially imitation. And to be even more precise, it's a contagious idea that's passed along—a mind virus."

"A mind virus?"

"Yes. A mind virus. No different than any other viral contagion. The mind virus may be hosted in the minds of one or more individuals and can reproduce itself in the sense of jumping from the mind of one person to the mind of another, reproducing itself in a new host."

"And how does this pertain to the missing children?"

"They were infected by a dreadful virus."

"Infected? What did you see?"

"I saw the infection as it occurred."

"I'm confused. You're saying that they were infected by a funny picture?"

"No. Of course not. Sure, a mind virus can be spread by social media or email, but it can also be spread by word-of-mouth. That's what happened to the children, it's what was said to them that infected them, what they repeated. A children's playground song."

"A nursery rhyme?"

"No. Nursery rhymes are learned in childhood then when the child reaches adulthood, they pass it on to more children. Children's playground songs are learned and passed on almost immediately. A jump-rope song, for example, like 'Miss Lucy.' Do you know 'Miss Lucy'?"

"Oh, sure. We sang that when I was a girl. Miss Lucy had baby. Yes, I remember it. There was another one too, a different version, 'Miss Susie,' that my mother didn't like very well."

"You remember how you learned them, those songs?"

"No. No I don't. It was just something we sang with double dutch. I suppose I learned it from the other girls. We used to practice with our hands, clapping, going faster and faster."

"Exactly. It was passed on to you by children who learned it from other children. Would you believe me if I told you that children were teaching it to each other as far back as the nineteenth century, from European variations even older than that?"

"I guess I never thought about it."

"You know, that section of the university where I live is over two hundred years old. It was built over the ruins of an indigenous village. The playground itself was later built in a public area where public executions were held. Criminals were hung from the university walls."

"I didn't know that."

"Have you ever heard of Elsie Doolittle?"

"Wasn't she burned as a witch?"

"Well, you're half right. She was hanged. One of the public executions. The children made a song about it."

"I see. And you're saying that children's song has been passed along for two hundred years."

"Yes."

"And that it's one of these memes—a mind virus."

"That's right. It's been living in the playground, infecting children generation after generation."

"And you believe it infected Sophia Carmichael and Lyndon Christensen?"

"I told you, I saw it happen."

"Okay. So, say that something was said to these children that affected them in some way. Some trigger words that made them run away. If that were true, if this rhyme has been living in the playground for two hundred years, why hasn't there been other disappearances? How could this 'virus' be passed down and only now affect someone?"

"All of these songs—'Hello Operator', 'Miss Lucy', 'Miss Susie', 'Miss Elsie'—have all changed. They modify as the words and phrases are forgotten, misunderstood or updated."

"Exactly. Why would a two-hundred-year-old rhyme matter now?"

"Because the virus has waited for the right time to revert the lyrics."

"You're saying the virus, I mean the rhyme, changed itself."

"I told you, that section of the university was built on an indigenous village, on their burial ground. There's power there, enough to keep the contagion alive, to keep her alive. Maybe she whispered the change herself. You said this is the first time it's happened here, and that's simply not true. This isn't the first time. It happened forty years ago, when I was a girl. And, if you check, you'll see it happened forty years before that, then further before that, going back to when she first took the children."

"She?"

"Why, Elsie, of course. Elsie Doolittle."

"You're saying a two-hundred-year-old witch took the children."

"Oh yes. That's how she was found out, what she was hanged for. Taking two children."

"And where did she take them?"

"I told you, I don't exactly know. But I'd bet that if you look in the archives, you may find a clue as to where she took the others, where you'll find Sophia and Lyndon."

"Larry, could you please go check to see what we have in the archives? And I'll keep Professor Blackburne company, until you get back."

ABOUT THE AUTHORS

Hunter C. Eden is a Denver-based essayist and dark fantasy writer whose work has appeared in **Weird Tales**, **City Slab**, and **Ravenous Monster Horror Webzine**.

Lara Frater, published a non-fiction book *Fat Chicks Rule! How to Survive a Thin Centric World*. It was a guidebook on being a big girl in a thin world and included information on how to fat positive books, movies, and TV, where to find fashion, comfortable seating, and how to deal with fat hatred. A few months after the book was published, I did a companion blog with the same name that she still updates every Monday.

She has published essays, poetry and short stories.

In 2012, she published *End of the Line* the first in the series of three zombie novels that take place in a world almost dead of the flu and having to deal the zombies who rose from the ashes. *End of the Line* was followed by *Stuck in the Middle* in 2013 and *Full Circle* in 2014.

She is also working on a three book dystopian series called *Welcome to Pluto*. I hope to have the first book out in 2016.

She lives in New York City with her husband, author Jonathan Frater and has lots of animals and people in her house.

C.C. Ameel lives in Michigan with her husband, Jon, and son, Seth. She enjoys loud music, scary movies, and studying the criminal mind. She spends time writing when she should be sleeping, finding the brightest inspiration comes during the darkest hours.

Ian Garner is an award-winning actor and author from Mississippi. He received the Gold Key Award for his short story, *Forevermore,* in the Scholastic Regional Writing Competition in April 2014. He is the author of *Whispers, American Son, Roswell,* and most recently, *Home*. Ian is pursuing a degree in education and plans to write many more stories in the near future.

Jessica West (a.k.a. West1Jess) is currently pursuing a state of self-induced psychosis, also known as writing. In the past, she has worked for Wal-Mart, a lawyer, and a bank. Now if she could just get a couple years experience with the IRS and the NSA, world domination is in the bag.

Jess lives in Acadiana with three daughters still young enough to think she's cool and a husband who knows better but likes her anyway.

For more information, visit west1jess.com

Daniel Arthur Smith is a USA Today bestselling author. His titles include *Spectral Shift, Hugh Howey Lives, The Cathari Treasure, The Somali Deception*, and a few other novels and short stories. He also curates the phenomenal short fiction series *Tales from the Canyons of the Damned* and *Frontiers of Speculative Fiction*.

He was raised in Michigan and graduated from Western Michigan University where he studied philosophy, with focus on cognitive science, meta-physics, and comparative religion. He began his career as a bartender, barista, poetry house proprietor, teacher, and then became a technologist and futurist for the Fortune 100 across the Americas and Europe.

Daniel has traveled to over 300 cities in 22 countries, residing in Los Angeles, Kalamazoo, Prague, Crete, and now writes in Manhattan where he lives with his wife and young sons.

For more information, visit danielarthursmith.com

www.ingramcontent.com/pod-product-compliance
Lightning Source LLC
Chambersburg PA
CBHW020602130626
46552CB00007B/3003